DREAMS OF ROSES

KENZIE SKYE

ONE

The winding dirt road stretches on with no end in sight, twisting through a thick forest that seems to close in around me. I check the crumpled delivery slip again, but it offers no answers. Just a vague address that led me into this forgotten corner of the city outskirts.

Ferns and mossy branches spill onto the narrow road ahead. I ease my delivery van forward, tires crunching on gravel and debris. The canopy grows denser overhead, filtering the sunlight into mottled shadows that dance across the windshield.

"Of course the address would be impossible to find," I mutter, glancing at the elaborate bouquet of calla lilies and roses in the passenger seat. The arrangement took me hours to perfect. But this eerie, isolated route makes me question who the recipient could be.

I round another bend and step on the brakes with a gasp. Rising from a sea of fog and overgrowth looms an enormous stone mansion, materializing like an apparition. Gothic spires spiral into the sky and dark vines devour the facade. The remnants of what may have once been an impressive estate now stand draped in neglect and mystery.

Something in my gut tells me to turn around. That this detour into an eerie unknown can lead nowhere good. I think of the work waiting for me at the flower shop, how I need to be back in time to prepare bouquets for the Midsummer's Eve festival. My tummy rumbles as I think of a warm cinnamon rolls and a hot cup of chai tea.

But as I gaze at the enigmatic mansion through the swirling mist, a magnetic pull draws me in, whispering of secrets waiting to unfurl. Maybe the intended recipient of this special bouquet is inside, lost and alone. Maybe they need someone to find them as much as I need answers to sate my growing curiosity about this place.

I switch off the ignition and grab the flowers, fingers trembling slightly as I push open the van door. A gust of damp, earthy air envelops me. The mansion looms closer through a veil of fog, imposing and almost sinister. But also...inviting, in an inexplicable way that both frightens and thrills me.

Leaves crunch under my boots as I approach the weathered steps, bracing for the unknown that surely awaits within. A shiver ripples down my spine, but I press on, determined to unravel this mystery one way or another. The enormous oak doors beckon, daring me to discover what lies on the other side.

With a deep breath to steel my nerves, I raise a hand to knock.

As my knuckles graze the weathered wood, the door swings open with an ominous creak. I step back, heart pounding in my chest, as a figure emerges from the shadows. Tall and imposing, he fills the doorway, his piercing blue eyes fixed upon me with an intensity that steals my breath.

"Who are you?" His voice is deep, laced with a mix of suspicion and intrigue. "And what business do you have trespassing on my property?"

Holy fuck, this dude is scary.

I swallow hard, my grip tightening on the bouquet. "I-I'm Bonnie Flowers. I was trying to deliver these, but I got lost and-"

"You shouldn't be here." He steps forward, his

presence both fearsome and magnetic. "This is no place for a curious little flower like you."

Despite the warning in his tone, I stand my ground. "I apologize for the intrusion, but I couldn't just leave without ensuring these flowers reached their intended recipient."

A flicker of something—amusement, perhaps?—dances in his eyes. "And you thought it wise to explore a stranger's home uninvited?"

Heat rushes to my cheeks. "I didn't mean any harm. I'll leave now if you just point me in the right direction."

He regards me for a long moment, his gaze penetrating, as if he can see straight into my soul. Then, a smile curves his lips, but it's far from reassuring. "I'm afraid it's not that simple, little flower. You've seen too much already."

My heart stutters. "What do you mean?"

He steps closer, his presence overwhelming, his scent a heady mix of forest and something distinctly masculine. "You've trespassed on my domain, and now, you must face the consequences."

Before I can react, he seizes my wrist, his touch searing my skin. "You'll be staying here, as my prisoner, until I deem fit to release you."

Panic surges through me, mingling with a traitorous thrill at his proximity. "You can't do this! I have a life, a job-"

"Not anymore." His words are final, unyielding. "The moment you crossed that threshold, your fate was sealed."

As he drags me inside, the bouquet tumbles from my grasp, petals scattering like lost dreams on the cold stone floor. The door slams shut behind us with a resounding finality, and I'm left to wonder if I've just stumbled into a fairy tale...

Or a nightmare from which there is no escape.

Two

I run my fingers over the silky sheets, marveling at the lavish furnishings that adorn my gilded cage. The four-poster bed looms large, its velvet canopy draping elegantly from above. Intricate tapestries depicting mythical beasts and enchanted forests cover the stone walls, their threads seeming to whisper secrets of a world beyond my understanding.

As I explore the room, my eyes are drawn to an ornate mirror hanging above the fireplace. Its frame is adorned with delicate roses carved from gleaming silver, their petals so lifelike I half expect to catch their scent. I approach cautiously, my reflection wavering in the ancient glass. For a moment, I swear I see a flicker of movement behind me—a shadow with piercing blue eyes.

I whirl around, heart pounding, but the room is empty. The eerie sensation lingers, making me question the nature of my surroundings. This is no ordinary mansion. There's magic woven into its very foundations, ancient and powerful.

A soft knock at the door startles me from my reverie. I tense, knowing it can only be *him*, my captor and the master of this strange realm.

The door creaks open, revealing his imposing figure. He fills the doorway, his broad shoulders casting shadows across the room. His dark hair falls in waves around a face that might have been handsome once, before bitterness etched itself into every line.

"You will join me for dinner," he commands, his voice low and gruff. It's not a request.

I swallow hard, my mouth suddenly dry. "I'm not hungry," I manage to say, my voice trembling slightly.

His eyes narrow. "It wasn't a question."

I feel the weight of his gaze upon me, intense and unrelenting. Fear coils in my stomach, but beneath it, something else stirs—a curiosity, a strange pull towards this enigmatic man.

He studies me for a long moment, as if trying to unravel a puzzle. "You will dine with me," he repeats, his tone softening almost imperceptibly. "Please."

The unexpected word hangs in the air between us. I nod slowly, unsure of what to make of this small concession.

As he turns to leave, I catch a glimpse of something in his eyes—a flicker of longing, perhaps even vulnerability. It's gone in an instant, replaced by hardness.

The door closes behind him with a resounding thud, leaving me alone once more in this luxurious prison. I sink onto the bed, my mind reeling.

I glance at the mirror again, half expecting to see those haunting blue eyes staring back at me. Instead, I find only my own reflection, a girl far from home, in a mess and with no foreseeable way to get out.

I jump when there's a soft knock at the door. An old woman dressed in a maid's outfit enters. She smiles at me kindly and tells me she'll escort me to dinner.

"Who is the owner of this place? Where am I?" I grill her for answers.

She averts her eyes and doesn't answer my first quesiton. "Thornfield Manor," she says simply.

"How do I get out of here? He's kidnapped me. I'm not here of my own free will," I tell her desperately.

She wrings her hands nervously and refuses to

meet my eyes as she assures me, "Now, now, miss. The master won't hurt you. I'm sure of it."

Master? It's like I've traveled back in time or something. Who refers to their employer as master?

"Come now," she urges me gently.

I follow because somehow I have a feeling running wouldn't do any good. This man, whoever he is, surely has enough sense to have all the doors locked. If he said I'm his prisoner, I have no doubt that I won't be released until he's good and ready.

The old maid leads me through a labyrinth of dimly lit corridors, the flickering candlelight casting eerie shadows on the walls. We pass by ancient portraits, their eyes seeming to follow our every step. The air grows colder as we descend a grand staircase, and I shiver, pulling my shawl tighter around my shoulders.

At last, we arrive at a set of heavy wooden doors, intricately carved with scenes of mythical creatures engaged in an eternal dance. The maid pushes them open, revealing a vast dining room that takes my breath away.

Crystal chandeliers hang from the vaulted ceiling, casting a soft glow over the long mahogany table that dominates the space. The table is set for two, with fine china and gleaming silverware that sparkle in the candlelight. A grand fireplace crackles at the far end of the room, its mantel adorned with intricate carvings of roses and thorns.

And there, standing at the head of the table, is *him*. He cuts an imposing figure in his dark tailored suit, his broad shoulders and tall frame filling the space with a commanding presence. His piercing blue eyes meet mine, and I feel a shiver run down my spine.

I step forward, my footsteps echoing on the polished marble floor. "Who are you?" I demand, my voice sounding small in the vastness of the room. "What is your name?"

A flicker of amusement crosses his face. "Cade Thornfield," he replies, his voice low and smooth like velvet. "And you, Bonnie Flowers, are my guest."

I freeze, my heart pounding in my chest. "How do you know my name?"

He doesn't answer, instead gesturing to the chair beside him. "Please, sit. Dinner will be served shortly."

I hesitate, torn between the desire to flee and the strange pull I feel towards this enigmatic man. Slowly, I approach the table and take my seat, the plush velvet cushion enveloping me in its warmth.

Cade takes his place at the head of the table, his

gaze never leaving mine. The firelight dances across his face, casting shadows that accentuate the sharp angles of his cheekbones and the fullness of his lips.

A sudden gust of wind rattles the windows, and the candles flicker, casting eerie shadows on the walls. For a moment, I swear I see the shadows take on a life of their own, writhing and twisting like tortured souls.

I blink, and the illusion is gone, leaving only the steady glow of the candles and the intensity of Cade's gaze upon me.

"You haven't answered my question," I say, my voice trembling slightly. "How do you know who I am?"

Cade leans back in his chair, a ghost of a smile playing at the corners of his mouth. "I have my ways," he replies cryptically. "Let's just say that I've been...expecting you."

I frown, unease prickling at the back of my neck. "Expecting me? What do you mean? Why am I here?"

He reaches for the decanter of wine, pouring a deep crimson liquid into his glass. The rich aroma wafts through the air, mingling with the scent of the roaring fire. "All in good time, Bonnie. For now, let us enjoy this meal together."

As if on cue, servants emerge from the shadows, bearing trays laden with sumptuous dishes. They set the plates before us, revealing a feast fit for royalty—succulent roasted meats, vibrant seasonal vegetables, and exotic fruits I've never seen before.

Despite the enticing spread, my appetite eludes me. I can't shake the feeling that there's more to Cade's words, a hidden meaning lurking beneath the surface.

I pick at my food, my mind spinning with questions. Cade, on the other hand, seems perfectly at ease, savoring each bite with an almost sensual pleasure. His eyes flick to mine, catching me staring.

"Is the food not to your liking?" he asks, arching an eyebrow.

I set down my fork, meeting his gaze head-on. "Why am I really here, Cade? You can't expect me to sit here and play along with this charade without any explanation."

His lips curve into a smirk. "Ah, there it is. The fire I sensed in you from the moment you arrived."

He rises from his seat, moving around the table with a predatory grace. As he draws closer, I catch a hint of his scent—something dark and earthy, with a hint of spice. It's intoxicating and unsettling all at once.

"You're here because fate has brought you to me," he murmurs, his breath tickling my ear. "Because we are bound by a connection that runs deeper than you can possibly imagine."

I shiver, my skin prickling with goosebumps. "I don't understand..."

His fingers ghost along my jawline, tilting my face up to meet his intense gaze. "You will, in time. But for now, all you need to know is that you belong here, with me."

The air between us crackles with tension, a heady mix of fear and something else, something I dare not name. I'm drawn to him like a moth to a flame, even as every instinct screams at me to run.

Cade's eyes darken, as if he can sense my inner turmoil. "Don't fight it, Bonnie," he whispers, his lips a hairsbreadth from mine. "Embrace the destiny that has brought you into my

Cade's lips hover dangerously close to mine, his breath hot against my skin. I tremble, torn between the urge to pull away and the magnetic pull drawing me toward him.

"I don't believe in destiny," I manage to whisper, my voice unsteady. "You can't keep me here against my will."

A dark chuckle rumbles in his chest. "Oh, but I

can. You'll come to see things my way...in time." His fingers skim down the side of my neck, leaving a trail of fire in their wake.

I jerk back, glaring at him. "I'm not some possession for you to claim. I have a life, people who will be looking for me."

Cade's eyes glint with amusement. "Do you now? And who might that be? From what I've gleaned, you're quite...alone in this world."

Ice trickles down my spine at his words. How much does he know about me? Has he been watching me, studying my life from the shadows? The thought makes me feel exposed, violated.

"You don't know anything about me," I snap, pushing away from the table. The chair scrapes harshly against the marble floor as I stand, facing him defiantly.

In a flash, Cade is on his feet, his tall frame looming over me. He grasps my chin firmly, forcing me to meet his penetrating gaze.

"I know enough. I know the loneliness that plagues you, the yearning for something more. I know the fire that burns within you, begging to be unleashed." His voice is low, seductive, weaving a spell that threatens to ensnare me.

I try to turn my face away but his grip tightens,

his fingers digging into my skin. "Let me go," I hiss through clenched teeth.

A slow, wicked smile spreads across his lips. "Never. You're mine now, little flower. Best get used to it."

With that, he crushes his mouth against mine in a bruising kiss. I gasp and he takes advantage, his tongue delving deep to claim me. I taste wine and forbidden desire, a heady combination that makes my knees weak.

Some base instinct takes over and I find myself returning the kiss, my fingers tangling in his silky hair. Cade groans, pulling my body flush against his. I can feel the hard, hot length of him pressing insistently against my stomach.

Shame and lust war within me as his hands roam possessively down my curves to grip my ass. He kneads the soft globes, grinding his hips in a dirty promise of things to come.

No! This is madness. With a burst of clarity, I wrench myself out of his arms, stumbling back. Cade looks startled for a split second before his eyes narrow dangerously.

"This isn't over," he growls.

I pant heavily, my heart racing as I stare at Cade in shock. His eyes bore into mine, dark with lust and something far more dangerous.

"I won't be your plaything," I manage to choke out, my voice trembling despite my best efforts to sound firm. "Whatever twisted game this is, I refuse to participate."

Cade stalks towards me, a predatory gleam in his gaze. I back away until I collide with the cold stone wall. He cages me in with his arms, his body a hot, hard line against mine.

"Oh, my sweet Bonnie," he murmurs, his breath ghosting over my lips. "This is no game. You were meant to be mine, don't you see? The fates have woven our threads together, binding us in ways you can't begin to fathom."

His words send a shiver down my spine, even as my treacherous body responds to his closeness. I feel drawn to him, like a moth to a flame, despite every instinct screaming at me to flee.

"You're delusional," I whisper, my voice cracking. "I don't belong to you or anyone else."

Cade chuckles darkly, his hand coming up to caress my cheek with a gentleness that belies the intensity in his eyes. "We shall see about that, little flower. In time, you'll come to crave my touch, to yearn for me with every fiber of your being."

His thumb traces the outline of my lower lip,

and I shudder, my breath hitching in my throat. He leans in closer, his lips a hair's breadth from mine.

Just then, a loud clap of thunder echoes through the room, making me jump. Cade tenses, his head snapping towards the window. The sky outside is an ominous shade of grey, heavy clouds roiling with the promise of a storm. The moon is almost full.

He steps back, releasing me from his hold. I sag against the wall, my legs trembling beneath me. Cade runs a hand through his dark hair, his jaw clenched tight.

"It seems our dinner has been cut short," he says, his voice low and strained. "I have matters to attend to. Esmerelda will show you back to your room."

The old maid appears as if summoned, her eyes downcast as she curtsies. "Come, miss," she murmurs, gesturing for me to follow.

I hesitate, my gaze flicking back to Cade. He meets my eyes, a torrent of emotions swirling in their depths—longing, frustration, and something akin to regret.

"Until tomorrow, Bonnie," he says softly, a promise and a warning all at once.

I allow Esmerelda to lead me from the room, my mind reeling from the events of the evening.

What the hell?

THREE

I drift into a fitful sleep, the events of the day playing behind my eyelids like a flickering shadow play. The scent of roses, thick and cloying, fills my nostrils as I find myself standing in a vast garden. Thornfield Manor looms in the distance, its stone walls covered in a tangled web of vines and thorns.

Before me, a path unfurls, lined with roses of every color imaginable. Their petals shimmer in the moonlight, each one a delicate masterpiece. I take a step forward, drawn by an inexplicable force.

As I move deeper into the garden, the roses begin to change. Their colors fade, petals withering and falling to the ground like tears. The once vibrant blooms now stand as mere shadows of their former glory, their stems gnarled and twisted.

A voice whispers on the wind, a familiar baritone that sends shivers down my spine. "The curse..." it breathes, "only you can break it."

I spin around, searching for the source of the voice, but find only the endless sea of dying roses. A sense of urgency grips me, a desperate need to understand the meaning behind this haunting vision.

"How?" I call out, my voice trembling. "How do I break the curse?"

The whispers intensify, swirling around me like a vortex of secrets. "Find the truth... beneath the thorns..."

I awaken with a gasp, my heart pounding against my ribcage. The lingering scent of roses fills the room, a ghostly reminder of the dream that felt so real. I sit up, my mind racing with questions and a newfound determination.

I clutch the silken sheets, my heart hammering against my ribs as the remnants of the dream cling to my mind. The scent of dying roses lingers, a haunting reminder of the mysterious curse that plagues this place. Thornfield Manor holds secrets, dark and ancient, and somehow I've become entwined in its twisted web.

Slowly, I rise from the bed, my bare feet sinking into the plush carpet. I pace the room, trying to make sense of the cryptic message from my dream. Find the truth beneath the thorns...What could it mean?

My thoughts drift to Cade, the enigmatic master of this gothic prison. The memory of his lips on mine, demanding and possessive, sends a shiver down my spine. I can still feel the heat of his touch, the way his strong hands gripped my body as if he owned me. A traitorous part of me aches to feel that scorching passion again, even as my mind recoils in disgust.

No, I can't let him get under my skin. I need to find a way out of here, to unravel the mystery that binds me to this accursed place. But where do I even begin?

A soft knock at the door startles me from my ruminations. "Come in," I call out, my voice wavering slightly.

Esmerelda enters, carrying a silver tray laden with breakfast delicacies. The aroma of freshly baked bread and spiced tea wafts through the air, making my stomach grumble despite my unease.

"Good morning, miss," the old maid greets me,

her kind eyes crinkling at the corners. "I hope you slept well."

I force a smile, not wanting to burden her with my troubled thoughts. "As well as can be expected, given the circumstances."

She sets the tray down on the bedside table, her movements precise and practiced. "The master has requested your presence in the library after you've eaten. He wishes to speak with you."

My pulse quickens at the mention of Cade. Part of me wants to refuse, to barricade myself in this room and shut out his dark allure. But I know I can't hide forever. If I'm going to uncover the truth about Thornfield Manor and the curse that haunts it, I'll need to confront him.

"Very well," I reply, steeling my resolve. "Please inform him that I will join him shortly."

Esmerelda nods, a flicker of something akin to sympathy in her gaze. "Take heart, miss. The master may be a complicated man, but I believe there is goodness in him, buried deep beneath the thorns."

With those cryptic words, she takes her leave, shutting the door softly behind her. I stare after her, wondering how much she knows about the secrets of this place.

I pick at the breakfast offerings, my appetite diminished by the knots in my stomach.

I force myself to eat a few bites, knowing I'll need my strength for whatever lies ahead. The food is exquisite, but it tastes like ashes in my mouth.

Once I've eaten my fill, I dress quickly in a simple yet elegant gown left out for me—no doubt by Esmerelda. I mean, it's beautiful, but it feels like something from another century. Nobody dresses this way anymore. The deep emerald fabric complements my auburn hair and brings out the green in my eyes. I feel like I'm donning armor for battle as I fasten the tiny buttons.

Steeling my spine, I venture out into the labyrinthine halls of Thornfield Manor. Though I've only been here a short while, my feet seem to know the way, guiding me through the twists and turns until I find myself before the imposing doors of the library.

I raise my hand to knock, but the door swings open of its own accord. Cade stands on the other side, devastatingly handsome in a crisp white shirt and dark trousers. His eyes rake over me, a mixture of hunger and something softer that makes my breath catch.

"Bonnie," he greets me, his voice a sinful caress.

"Thank you for joining me." He steps back, allowing me to enter.

The library is magnificent—towering bookcases filled with ancient tomes, plush armchairs positioned before a roaring fireplace, the air heavy with the scent of leather and old parchment. But I scarcely have time to take it in before Cade is prowling towards me, his movements fluid and graceful.

"I trust you slept well?" he inquires, though the wicked glint in his eye tells me he's perfectly aware of how fitfully I passed the night.

"Well enough," I reply coolly, determined not to let him see how deeply he affects me. "Your maid said you wished to speak with me."

"Indeed." He gestures for me to take a seat and I perch on the edge of a velvet sofa, my muscles tense. Cade remains standing, looming over me. "I thought it time we had a frank discussion about your role here."

I tip my chin up defiantly. "I don't have a role here. You're keeping me prisoner."

A ghost of a smile plays at his sensual mouth. "Prisoner is such an ugly word. I prefer to think of you as...a treasured guest."

"Call it what you will, the fact remains that I'm

here against my will," I fire back. "What gives you the right to hold me captive?"

Cade's eyes flash, a hint of that simmering danger beneath the surface. He leans down, caging me in with his arms braced on either side of my head. I'm engulfed in his intoxicating scent, a mix of sandalwood and raw masculinity. "You are here because it is your destiny, Bonnie. The fates have chosen you, just as they chose me."

I stare into Cade's intense blue eyes, my heart pounding against my ribcage. His words echo in my mind—the fates have chosen me. But for what? What twisted destiny could have possibly led me to this dark, mysterious man and his haunted manor?

"I don't believe in fate," I whisper, my voice trembling slightly. "And even if I did, I wouldn't blindly accept being held here against my will, no matter what the reason."

Cade's lips curve into a humorless smile. "Defiant little flower, aren't you? But you're only fighting the inevitable. There are forces at work here beyond your understanding."

He straightens, giving me room to breathe again, but I still feel trapped by the sheer magnetism of his presence. I watch warily as he paces over to the window, staring out at the wild, tangled gardens below.

"You dreamed of the rose garden last night, didn't you?" he asks without turning around.

I inhale sharply. How could he possibly know that?

"I...I don't know what you're talking about," I stammer, but the lie sounds feeble even to my own ears.

Cade looks back at me over his shoulder, his gaze knowing. "Don't bother denying it. I felt your consciousness brush against mine as you walked among the blooms in your mind. You heard the whispers, felt the curse that lies heavy over this place."

A chill skitters down my spine. The dream had felt so real, so visceral. And now Cade spoke of it as if he'd been there with me, as if our minds were somehow connected.

"What are you?" I breathe, half afraid to hear the answer. "What is this curse you speak of and what does it have to do with me?"

Cade turns fully to face me, his expression inscrutable. "I am a man bound by fate and magic, Bonnie. Cursed to walk this earth until I fulfill my destiny. And you..." He takes a step towards me, his eyes blazing with an emotion I dare not name. "You are the key to everything. Only you have the power to break the curse and set me free."

I shake my head in denial, even as some deep, hidden part of me responds to his words with a flicker of recognition. "This is madness. Curses, destiny, fated keys...those things don't exist outside of fairy tales."

"Oh, I assure you, this is no fairy tale," Cade murmurs silkily as he stalks closer, a predator scenting his prey. "The magic that flows through Thornfield is ancient and dark, and it will not be denied."

He's close now, close enough that I can feel the unnatural heat radiating from his body. His hand comes up to grip my chin, forcing me to meet his burning gaze.

"Don't fight it, Bonnie," he urges, his voice a seductive purr. "The connection between us is undeniable. You feel it too, don't you? The pull, the yearning deep in your core..."

His words wash over me like a drugging caress, making me sway towards him. It would be so easy to give in, to let him claim me body and soul. But some small, stubborn part of me resists, clinging to sanity.

I jerk my chin out of his grasp and stumble back

a step. "No," I rasp, shaking my head to clear the sensual fog.

He scowls before he finally throws up a hand in frustration. "Go back to your room then."

I stand there stupidly, frozen.

"Go!" he finally roars, and the sound is so loud and frightening that I immediately obey, my feet carrying me back to my room as fast as they can.

I slam the door behind me and then lean back on it, my heart galloping in my chest.

What kind of psychopath is he?

Four

Heart pounding, I tiptoe through the shadowy corridors of Thornfield Manor, searching for any way out of this eerie labyrinth. The ancient floorboards groan beneath my feet as I pass faded tapestries and weathered portraits that seem to watch my every move with haunting eyes.

A faint light flickers ahead, spilling from the half-open door of the library. Curiosity draws me forward, even as some primal instinct whispers a warning. I peer through the gap.

There, in a grand wing-backed chair, sits Cade Thornfield himself. But he's not reading as one might expect. No, the formidable master of the manor has his trousers undone, his hand wrapped around his thick, rigid shaft as he strokes himself with languid purpose. Shadows dance across the sharp planes of his face, highlighting the intense rapture in his expression.

I should look away. I should flee before he notices my intrusion. Yet I find myself frozen, transfixed by the erotic display before me. It's wrong, so very wrong to keep watching, but a small, secret part of me thrills at the forbidden sight.

"Bonnie," Cade suddenly gasps, his rich baritone sending a shiver down my spine.

Piercing blue eyes snap open and collide with mine. Mortification floods through me at being caught, but Cade holds my gaze steadily, unabashed. If anything, the sight of me only seems to further enflame his desire.

His hand continues its sensual motion, each measured stroke bringing him closer to release. I know I should run, but my feet feel rooted in place, my breath caught in my throat as the air crackles with a dangerous sort of tension.

Cade's eyes blaze into mine, raw with lust and something else I can't quite name. Faster now, his fist pumps along his impressive length, a bead of sweat trickling down his temple. The sound of skin against skin and his increasingly ragged breaths fill the room, drowning out the wild hammering of my own heartbeat.

Then, with a guttural groan that resonates deep in my core, Cade comes. I gasps as I watch it. His powerful body goes rigid as he spills his release over his fist in thick, white ropes, his penetrating gaze never once leaving mine.

It's odd because I'm the one who caught him a vulnerable state, but *I* feel stripped bare before him, like he can see straight into the hidden depths of my soul and all the secret longings I keep locked away. It's thrilling and terrifying all at once.

Face burning, I finally break eye contact and flee back to the temporary safety of my room. Yet even as I hurry away, the searing memory of what I witnessed plays over and over in my mind, awakening a confusing mix of emotions I'm not quite ready to confront.

Alone in my chamber, I close the heavy door behind me and lean against it, trying to catch my breath. My heart races, and my pulse thrums in my ears as the adrenaline of the moment starts to wear off. I've never seen a man in such a state of undress, let alone witnessed something so...intimate.

Cade's face, flushed with desire, and his needy

moans replay themselves in my mind's eye, and despite my best efforts to chase them away, they only seem to grow stronger. Heat creeps into my cheeks as I admit to myself the primal part of me that found his unabashed lust...captivating.

And he was moaning *my* name.

But this is Cade we're talking about—my captor. I can't afford to get tangled up in whatever game he's playing. I've got to find a way out, not to let myself get caught up in his sick game of cat and mouse.

I open the door to resume my search and scream when I find Cade standing patiently on the other side of it.

"Going somewhere, little flower?" he growls down at me with a smirk.

I stumble back from the door, my heart leaping into my throat as Cade looms over me, his large frame filling the doorway. His eyes burn with an intensity that steals my breath, a predatory glint in their icy blue depths.

"I...I was just..." I stammer, my tongue suddenly feeling thick and clumsy in my mouth. How can I possibly explain my wanderings, or the fact that I witnessed his most private moment?

Cade steps into the room, closing the door

behind him with a decisive click. The sound echoes in my ears like the sealing of a tomb. He stalks towards me, each measured footfall sending a shiver down my spine.

"You were just what, Bonnie?" he purrs, his deep voice dripping with dark promise. "Snooping where you don't belong? Spying on things not meant for your innocent eyes?"

I back away until my legs hit the edge of the bed, forcing me to sit. Cade towers over me, his broad shoulders blocking out the dim candlelight. The air between us crackles with a dangerous electricity, and I'm suddenly all too aware of his masculine scent— woodsmoke and spice and something uniquely him.

"I didn't mean to," I whisper, my voice sounding breathless even to my own ears. "I got lost, and then I heard...I'm sorry, I shouldn't have looked."

Cade leans down, planting his hands on either side of me, his face mere inches from mine. I can feel the heat radiating off his body, seeping through my thin nightgown.

"But you did look, didn't you, little flower?" he murmurs, his breath ghosting across my lips. "You saw me in the throes of passion, stroking my cock as I moaned your name. Did you like what you saw?"

My cheeks flame hotly at his crude words, at the forbidden images they conjure. I want to deny it, to tell him I felt nothing, but the traitorous hammering of my pulse between my thighs gives me away.

Cade smirks knowingly, one large hand coming up to trace the delicate line of my jaw. His touch ignites sparks beneath my skin, and I have to bite back a whimper.

"Such a curious little thing," he muses, his thumb grazing the swell of my bottom lip. "I bet...you are a virgin." My face flames brighter because he's right. I am. "So innocent, yet so eager to learn the ways of pleasure. Shall I teach you, Bonnie? Shall I show you what it means to be worshipped by a man's hands, his mouth...his cock?"

His filthy words send liquid heat pooling low in my belly, and I squeeze my thighs together against the aching throb of need. This is wrong, so very wrong, but my traitorous body yearns for his touch, for the sinful delights he promises.

Cade's hand slides down my throat to cup my breast through the thin fabric of my nightgown. I gasp at the sudden intimate contact, my nipple pebbling beneath his hot palm. He kneads the soft flesh, sending sparks of pleasure radiating through my body.

"So responsive," he rumbles approvingly. "I've barely touched you and you're already trembling for me, aren't you little flower?"

I want to deny it, but a breathy moan escapes my lips as he rolls my nipple between his fingers, the sensation shooting straight to my core. Moisture pools between my thighs, dampening my undergarments.

Cade's other hand bunches up my nightgown, inching the fabric up my bare legs with agonizing slowness. His knuckles graze the sensitive skin of my inner thighs and I shudder, caught between the instinct to snap my legs closed and the desire to let them fall open wantonly.

"P-please," I whimper, hardly recognizing my own voice, breathy and needy. I'm not even sure what I'm begging for - for him to stop or to never stop touching me.

"Please what, Bonnie?" Cade coaxes darkly. "Use your words. Tell me what you need."

His fingers dance along the edge of my undergarments, teasing me with fleeting touches. I buck my hips restlessly, seeking more of that delicious friction.

"Touch me," I gasp out, too far gone to be embarrassed. "I need you to touch me...there."

Cade's eyes flash with carnal heat. "As my lady commands."

With one deft motion, he rips my undergarments away, fully exposing my most intimate parts to his hungry gaze. Before I can even process the shock, he cups my weeping sex possessively, his long fingers delving between the slick folds.

"Gods, you're so wet for me already," he groans appreciatively. "Dripping like a ripe peach. I wonder how you taste..."

He brings his glistening fingers to his lips, sucking my essence from them with relish. The sight is so erotic that I clench around nothing, a fresh gush of arousal leaking from my untried opening.

"Delicious," Cade pronounces with a wicked grin. "I'm going to feast on this sweet cunt until you scream for me, little Bonnie."

He sinks to his knees before me, shouldering my quivering thighs apart. I'm fully exposed to him now, my most intimate place spread and weeping for his attentions. A distant part of me knows I should feel ashamed, but all I can focus on is the pulsing ache in my core and the promise of relief in Cade's darkened eyes.

"So pretty and pink," he murmurs, his breath hot on my flesh.

I gasp as Cade's mouth descends on my exposed sex, his tongue delving between my slick folds. The sensation is unlike anything I've ever felt before - hot and wet and utterly indecent. I try to squirm away but his strong hands grip my thighs, holding me open for his ravenous feast.

"Ah ah, none of that now," he admonishes, his words muffled against my sensitive flesh. "You wanted me to touch you, so let me touch you. With my tongue."

He seals his lips around my throbbing pearl, suckling hard. I cry out, my hands flying to his hair, unsure if I want to push him away or pull him closer. Wave after wave of tingling pleasure radiates through me as he laps and sucks and nibbles, stoking the fire building low in my belly.

Cade groans as he tastes my arousal, the vibrations making me shudder. "Fuck, your cunt is delectable. I could eat this juicy peach for hours."

His filthy words only heighten my excitement, a fresh flood of moisture leaking from my untouched opening. Cade laps it up eagerly, his tongue delving inside me, stretching me open. The intrusion feels strange but so, so good, and I find myself rocking my hips against his face, chasing more of that exquisite friction.

"That's it, fuck yourself on my tongue," Cade encourages darkly. "Take what you need."

His hands roam up to palm my breasts as he feasts on me, tweaking my pebbled nipples almost painfully. The dual sensations have me writhing and keening, my thighs beginning to quake as the pressure inside me builds to an impossible peak.

"Cade," I pant desperately, tugging at his hair. "I feel—I need—oh god..."

"That's it, little Bonnie," he rumbles. "Come for me. Soak my face with your sweet honey."

He sucks hard on my clit, sliding two fingers deep inside my clenching channel, and I shatter. My climax crashes over me in a tidal wave of ecstasy, my sex pulsing and fluttering wildly around his invading digits as I cry out my pleasure.

Cade works me through it, lapping up my release as I tremble and buck against his face. Only when I collapse back onto the bed, boneless and spent, does he relent. He presses one last tender kiss to my sensitized flesh before rising to his feet, his chin and lips glistening obscenely with my juices.

I ought to be mortified by my wanton behavior, but I'm too satiated to care. Cade smirks down at me knowingly, his eyes still blazing with hunger.

"That was just a taste, little flower," he rasps.

I can't speak. All I can do is lay there and stare as he stands and readjusts himself before he walks to the door.

When he gets to it, he stops and throws over his shoulder, "Oh, and little flower?"

I hold my breath as his eyes meet mine.

"There is no escape."

FIVE

I stayed locked up in my room as long as I could stand. Now, I wander through the labyrinthian halls of Thornfield Manor, my fingertips tracing the weathered wood paneling as I walk. The portraits lining the walls whisper secrets as I pass, their eyes following me through the gloom. I pause before a painting of a medieval lord, his piercing blue gaze so familiar it makes my breath catch.

It's impossible...but the resemblance to Cade is uncanny.

Further down the corridor, an open door beckons. Inside is a study filled with ancient tomes and strange artifacts. A wilted rose, black as midnight, floats suspended in a bell jar on the desk. As I step closer, it begins to glow with an ethereal light.

Images flood my mind—thorny vines creeping over the manor walls, blood-red petals drifting on the wind. The rose from my dreams. It's connected to this place, to Cade, somehow.

"You shouldn't be in here," a deep voice growls behind me. I whirl to face Cade, his expression stormy.

"I'm sorry, I was just curious..." My words falter under his intense stare. "Cade, how old are you really? Those paintings...they look just like you."

He flinches almost imperceptibly. "Older than you can possibly imagine."

The realization hits me then—ageless portraits, the timeless aura of the house itself. "You're immortal," I breathe, puzzle pieces locking into place.

A mirthless chuckle. "A blessing and a curse."

"Are you...a vampire?"

Cade barks out a laugh, but there's no humor in it. "If only it were that simple. I would have driven a stake through my own heart centuries ago."

He stalks over to a cabinet, pouring amber liquid into two crystal glasses. "You want to know what I am." It's not a question.

He hands me a drink, his fingers brushing mine. I shiver.

We sit in tense silence for a moment. Then

slowly, haltingly, Cade begins to speak. "There was a woman. A beggar. She came to my door one winter's night seeking shelter from the cold. I was arrogant, foolish...I turned her away." His grip tightens on his glass, knuckles white. "She cursed me for my cruelty, doomed me to this half-life. By the time I realized my mistake, she had vanished."

I swallow hard, the liquor burning my throat. "That must have been...difficult. To see the world change around you while you stayed the same."

Cade meets my gaze, and for an instant his mask slips. Behind the anger and bitterness, I glimpse a soul-deep loneliness, a desperate yearning to connect. My heart aches for him, this man trapped between worlds.

The moment stretches taut between us before he looks away. "I don't need your pity," he snarls, but the venom in his tone rings hollow.

"It's not pity." I reach out tentatively, laying my hand over his. He stiffens but doesn't pull away. "No one should have to carry a burden like that alone."

We lapse into silence again, but this time, it feels almost companionable. A fragile understanding blooming in the midst of so many secrets still left unspoken.

Yet...I feel like Cade is holding back, like there's still some deeper truth yet to be revealed.

But for now, this is enough. A start to help me understand him and maybe why I'm here.

———

In the days that follow, something shifts between Cade and me. Though he remains guarded, there are moments when his icy exterior cracks, revealing glimpses of the man beneath. He tries a different approach. Instead of speaking cryptically about fate and trying to seduce me, he takes me on long walks through the sprawling gardens, where roses the color of blood climb over crumbling stone walls. Their heady scent fills the air, at once seductive and unsettling.

"They bloomed the night I was cursed," Cade tells me, running a finger along a thorn-studded stem. "A reminder of my sins." His voice is heavy with self-loathing.

I watch him carefully, trying to reconcile the bitter, angry man with the one who speaks so tenderly to his roses. "Sins can be forgiven," I say softly. "Everyone deserves a second chance."

He turns to me then, his blue eyes piercing. For a

heartbeat, I think he might reach for me, but instead he jerks away as if burned. "You don't know the things I've done." His tone is final, a door slamming shut.

I'm quiet for a long moment before I tentatively ask, "Are you ever going to let me go?"

He doesn't answer.

We keep walking until Cade's arm suddenly comes out to halt me.

"Never go into that wing," he growls.

I look ahead into the west wing of the house. "Why?" I ask.

He merely scowls at me and doesn't answer.

I look down at the forbidden wing, but he yanks me along the opposite direction.

Of course, I'm more curious than ever about it now.

What is he hiding?

———

The days begin to blur. I don't know how long I've been here, and I start to wonder if I'm losing my mind. Whispers echo down empty corridors. Shadows move in the corner of my eye.

And I keep thinking about the forbidden wing.

And then, I could be crazy. Maybe I'm just imagining it, but I think I start to notice that Cade seems to vanish whenever the moon grows full and fat in the sky. I won't see him for three days at a time when that happens.

What the actual fuck does that mean?

One night, I can't ignore it any longer. Moonlight spills through the windows, painting everything in shades of silver and shadow. I look up at the moon.

Full.

I swallow. My heartbeat thunders in my ears as I creep toward the forbidden wing, the one I've been warned away from. There's a pulsing energy in the air, a static charge that raises the hair on my arms.

I push open the door, my breath catching in my throat. Cade stands with his back to me, his body rigid and trembling. Something is wrong. The air feels too thick, too heavy. And then he turns, and the scream dies on my lips.

Where Cade once stood is a beast, a monstrous creature straight out of a nightmare. Fangs glint in the moonlight, and claws gouge deep furrows into the wooden floor. But it's the eyes that root me in place. Blue eyes, achingly familiar, filled with pain and despair.

"Cade?" I whisper, my voice cracking.

The beast lets out a howl that vibrates in my bones, a sound of pure anguish. And even as terror threatens to overwhelm me, my heart breaks for the tortured soul trapped within this monstrous form. *This* is the real curse. This is what Cade wasn't telling me.

And I know with sudden, blinding clarity that the real curse isn't the one that turns Cade into a beast. It's the one that's kept him chained in solitude and self-loathing, convinced he's unworthy of love or redemption.

The beast advances, his movements jerky and uncoordinated, as if he's warring with himself. "Are you happy now, Bonnie?" he snarls, his voice a guttural growl. "Is this what you wanted to see? The monster I truly am?"

I shake my head, tears blurring my vision. I can't speak, and I don't know what I would say even if I could.

I make a strangled sound, and he recoils at the noise as if I've struck him, his claws tearing at the air between us. "Get out," he growls, his voice low and menacing. "Get out before I do something we'll both regret."

Fear and heartbreak war within me, but the look

in his eyes tells me he's beyond reason. With a choked sob, I turn and flee, my footsteps echoing through the halls of Thornfield Manor.

I don't stop until I reach my room, slamming the door behind me and sliding the heavy bolt into place. My heart pounds in my chest, and I sink to the floor, my back pressed against the unyielding wood.

Tears stream down my face as the reality of what I've just witnessed sinks in. Cade is cursed. A beast trapped in a never-ending cycle of torment and despair.

I should hate him for what he's done. For the way he's kidnapped me and held me here against my will, but something within me almost wants to understand.

Oh, Cade.

Above my head, I hear an ominous click.

I go completely still as I realize what the sound was.

No!

I stand up and pound on the door, but I hear Cade's heavy footsteps retreating down the corridor, each one a hammer strike against my fragile hopes of freedom. He's locked me up inside this gilded cage.

Fuck!

How long is he going to keep me locked in here?

Six

Shadows lengthen as the hours melt into days, marked only by Esmerelda's silent deliveries of meals on silver trays. The food turns to ash in my mouth. I plead with her, my voice cracking. "Please, tell Cade I need to speak with him. It's important."

Her eyes dart away, but she nods. "I will pass along the message, miss."

Yet Cade never comes. The silence of Thornfield Manor presses in, thick and oppressive, until I fear I may suffocate under its weight. Despair winds thorny tendrils around my heart, choking out any embers of optimism.

Sleep becomes my only solace, an escape to dreamscapes where the impossible seems within reach. In slumber's embrace, I find myself walking an ancient path, rose petals soft beneath my bare feet. Ahead, an arch of thorns rises to block my way, vicious and unyielding.

Realization blooms like a bud unfurling in the morning light. The roses, delicate and alluring—they are me. And the thorns, sharp and foreboding—they are Cade.

I step forward, my fingertips grazing a thorn. It parts for me, a small miracle. One by one, the thorns relent, allowing me passage. And there, in the heart of the briars, a single rose glows with unearthly radiance.

My feelings for Cade, complex and ever-growing, are the key that could unlock his curse. If only he would let me in, let me show him the beauty that still exists within his tortured soul.

I wake with a gasp, the dream fading like mist under the sun. If only he would speak to me...

————

The creak of the door hinges shatters the silence, and my heart leaps into my throat. Cade stands in the doorway, his broad frame casting a shadow across the floor. Finally!

I rise to my feet, a thousand words poised on the tip of my tongue, but he speaks first.

"You're free to go," he says, his voice rough as gravel. "I won't keep you here any longer."

Shock ripples through me, followed by a swell of emotions I can't quite name. "Cade, I—"

He holds up a hand, stopping me. "Don't. Just...just go, Bonnie. Before I change my mind."

I stand there for a long moment, shocked. I don't know why I'm not sprinting toward the door. This is what I wanted. My freedom. Any sane woman would have already jetted out of here.

But...I can't.

I take a step forward, then another, until I'm standing mere inches from him. His gaze meets mine, stormy blue eyes filled with a tempest of pain and longing. In this moment, I see the man beneath the curse, the one who has been alone for so long, yearning for a touch of compassion.

He's not the beast he turns into, nor is he the unfeeling asshole he makes himself out to be.

Slowly, I raise my hand and cup his cheek, my thumb brushing against the coarse stubble. He flinches but doesn't pull away. "I'm not going anywhere," I whisper.

Before he can protest, I lean in and press my lips

to his. The kiss is soft, tentative, a question and an answer all at once.

And I know it's crazy, but nothing has ever felt righter. It feels like coming *home*.

For a heartbeat, Cade is still, and I fear I've misread everything. But then, with a groan that seems to come from the depths of his soul, he pulls me flush against him, deepening the kiss.

His touch ignites a fire within me, and I melt into his embrace. Our hands roam, desperate to map every inch of each other's bodies. We stumble backwards, a tangle of limbs and gasping breaths, until the back of my knees hit the bed.

Cade lowers me onto the mattress, his weight settling over me like a welcome blanket. In the heat of our passion, clothing is shed, barriers stripped away until there is nothing left but skin on skin. His touch is reverent, worshipful, as if he can't quite believe I'm real.

"Are you sure you want this?" he growls as he licks a path down the column of my throat, nibbling and biting. "Because once I start, I won't be able to stop, Bonnie. You'll be mine forever."

Forever.

The word echoes in my head, and I find myself

nodding. Yes, I'll be Cade's forever, for this is how it was always meant to be.

I feel the rumble of Cade's growl through my palm that's pressed against his chest as he captures my nipple in his mouth and suckles it, sending fire shooting straight to my core.

I arch my back, pressing my breasts further into Cade's hungry mouth as he lavishes attention on my sensitive nipples, licking and nibbling until I'm writhing beneath him. "Please Cade," I beg shamelessly, "I need you inside me. Now."

He releases my nipple with a wet pop and grins wickedly. "Patience, my sweet Bonnie. I'm going to worship every inch of your luscious body first." His large, calloused hands skim down my sides, igniting flames across my skin.

Cade dips his head, trailing open-mouthed kisses along the valley between my breasts, down the quivering plane of my stomach. I tangle my fingers in his dark hair, urging him lower to where I'm throbbing with need.

"Fuck, you smell divine," he groans as he nuzzles the curls at the apex of my thighs. "I bet you taste even better." Without warning, he licks a long, slow stripe up my soaked slit, and I nearly fly off the bed at the sensation.

"Oh God, yes!" I cry out as he feasts on my dripping cunt like a man starved, lapping and sucking at my sensitive folds. His talented tongue swirls around my aching clit and I see stars, my thighs trembling.

He slips one, then two thick fingers inside my tight channel, pumping in and out as he continues his relentless assault on my clit. The dual stimulation has me hurtling toward the edge embarrassingly fast.

"That's it, my rose, let go. Come all over my face," Cade commands gruffly before sealing his lips around my clit and sucking hard.

I shatter with a silent scream, my walls clamping down on his fingers as wave after wave of ecstasy crashes over me. He works me through it, lapping up my release like it's the finest nectar.

Before I can catch my breath, Cade surges up my body and notches the thick head of his cock at my entrance. "I can't wait any longer. I have to be inside you, have to claim you as mine."

"Yes, I'm yours, all yours!" I declare fervently, wrapping my legs around his hips.

With one powerful thrust, he sheaths himself to the hilt, stretching and filling me so perfectly. We both groan at the sublime union, savoring the feeling of our bodies joined as one.

Cade sets a deep, driving rhythm, hitting that

spot deep inside me that has me seeing stars with every snap of his hips. I cling to his broad shoulders, digging my nails into his skin as I lose myself to the intense pleasure.

Our bodies move together in a timeless dance of passion, slick with sweat, the wet sounds of our coupling filling the room. Pressure coils tighter and tighter until I'm clinging desperately to Cade, panting.

Cade's thrusts become more urgent, more primal, as he chases his own release. I can feel every ridge and vein of his thick cock dragging against my fluttering walls, stoking the flames higher.

"Touch yourself," he demands gruffly. "I want to feel you coming apart on my cock."

I obey, slipping a hand between our sweat-slicked bodies to rub tight circles around my throbbing clit. The added stimulation is almost too much to bear. Electric pleasure zings through my nerves and I throw my head back with a throaty moan.

"Fuck, just like that," Cade growls, pistoning his hips faster, driving into me with abandon. "Milk my cock, Bonnie. Soak it with your sweet cream."

His filthy words are my undoing. I detonate with a ragged scream, my pussy spasming almost violently around his plundering length. Through the haze of my own climax, I feel Cade swell inside me, stretching me impossibly fuller.

With a roar that shakes the very foundations of the mansion, he buries himself to the hilt one last time and erupts, painting my womb with jets of his molten seed. I cling to him as he rides out the after-shocks, our hearts galloping in sync.

In the aftermath, a sated silence settles over us like a cozy blanket. Cade gathers me in his strong arms and I burrow into his chest, listening to the steady thump of his heartbeat.

It's only then that I notice the change in the air. Gone is the oppressive weight of dark magic. In its place, warmth and light seem to emanate from every surface, chasing away the shadows.

"Cade, look," I whisper in awe, pointing to the window.

Outside, the overgrown gardens are transforming before our eyes. Gnarled vines retreat, lush grass sprouts from the earth, and rose bushes burst into bloom, their delicate petals unfurling to greet the sun. It's like watching a time lapse of nature reclaiming what was once lost.

"The curse," Cade says, his voice thick with wonder. "It's broken."

He meets my gaze then, and the love shining in

his eyes steals my breath. "You saved me, Bonnie. Your love, your light, it was the key all along. I can never thank you enough."

Tears of joy prick at the corners of my eyes. "You don't have to thank me, Cade. Loving you is as natural as breathing." I cup his face in my hands, marveling at the peace that has smoothed the lines of pain and regret. "This is only the beginning of our happily ever after."

And as our lips meet in a kiss filled with promise and hope, I know in my heart that this is where I'm meant to be. Wrapped in Cade's strong embrace, our bodies still joined in the most intimate way possible, I've never felt more complete. More whole.

Cade's hand slides into my messy hair, cupping the back of my head as he deepens the kiss. It's languid and sensual, a slow exploration now that the desperate edge of lust has been sated. For the moment, at least.

I can already feel the stirrings of renewed desire as Cade's semi-hard cock twitches inside me. We break apart, panting softly.

"Insatiable wench," Cade teases, nipping at my bottom lip. "I've created a monster."

"You love it," I retort with a grin, clenching my

inner muscles around him. He groans, his eyes fluttering shut.

"Fuck, you'll be the death of me, woman. But what a way to go." His voice is gravelly with lust.

We fall into each other again, hands grasping, mouths hungry. Cade rolls his hips, letting me feel every thick inch as he grows fully hard once more. My fingernails rake down his back as he starts to move in deep, powerful strokes that push me up the bed.

The second round is slower, more intense. Cade takes his time stoking the flames, building me up until I'm a writhing, mewling mess beneath him. His sinful mouth maps every curve and hollow, finding all my secret, sensitive spots.

When his fingers delve between my thighs to rub firm circles around my swollen clit, I see stars. My thighs begin to quake, heralding my approaching climax.

"That's it, my love," Cade rasps, his breath hot against my ear. "Let me feel you fall apart on my cock again. You're so fucking beautiful when you come."

His praise, his touch, his thick length hitting that perfect spot inside me—it's too much. I shatter with a raw scream, my cunt bearing down on him like a vice. Cade fucks me through it, never slowing his relentless pace.

"Fuck, Bonnie!" he roars as my rippling walls trigger his own release. He spurts deep inside me, adding to the claiming from earlier. I milk every last drop, reveling in the hot pulses of his seed.

We collapse together, thoroughly spent and satiated. Cade's weight is a welcome blanket. I run my fingers through his damp hair as we catch our breath, trading soft kisses and even softer words of devotion.

Eventually, reluctantly, Cade slips free of my body. We both groan at the loss. Evidence of our coupling trickles down my thighs and Cade watches raptly, masculine satisfaction etched across his handsome face.

He pulls me to his chest, and as we lie entwined, our hearts beating in sync, I trace patterns on his chest, connecting the constellations of his scars. "I'm not going anywhere," I tell him, knowing that he needs to hear it, my voice a solemn vow. "I'm exactly where I'm meant to be."

And for the first time since I stepped foot in Thornfield Manor, I feel the stirrings of hope, delicate as a rosebud unfurling in the dawn.

SEVEN

The ballroom of Thornfield Manor glows with the flicker of a hundred candles, casting dancing shadows across the faces of our guests. Cade stands beside me, his presence both comforting and electrifying. Our fingers lace together as we survey the crowd, an eclectic mix of humans and mythical folk alike.

"Who knew integrating into the modern world would be such an affair," Cade murmurs, the hint of a smile playing at his lips. His eyes meet mine and my breath catches. Even after all we've been through, his gaze still stirs something deep within me.

I squeeze his hand. "We've earned this celebration. A new beginning, together." The words taste sweet on my tongue, a promise of the future we've fought so hard for.

As the night wears on, the music swells and laughter echoes off the ancient walls. Cade's hand finds the small of my back, his touch searing through the delicate fabric of my gown. He leans in close, his breath warm against my ear. "Meet me in the library in five minutes."

My heart races as I watch him slip away, his tall form disappearing into the shadows. I make my excuses, weaving through the throng of well-wishers until I reach the heavy wooden doors of the library.

Inside, the air is thick with the scent of old books and anticipation. Cade emerges from behind a towering shelf, his blue eyes darkened with desire. "Bonnie," he breathes, and then his lips are on mine, urgent and demanding.

We stumble backwards, hands grasping at clothes and tangling in hair. The rough edge of a table digs into my back as Cade lifts me onto it, scattering books and papers. His fingers skim up my thighs, pushing aside silk and lace. I gasp as he presses against me, the evidence of his want unmistakable.

"I need you," Cade growls, nipping at the sensitive skin of my throat. "Now. Always."

"Then take me," I whisper, surrendering to the force of our passion. Cade growls as he frees his rock-hard cock from his slacks. It springs free, angry and purple and with moisture beading the tip.

I moan as Cade teases my dripping entrance with the swollen head of his manhood. "Please Cade, I need you inside me," I beg, my voice breathy with desire.

With a primal grunt, he thrusts into me, stretching and filling me deliciously. The sensation is exquisite, his thick shaft hitting depths that make me see stars. I wrap my legs around his waist, urging him even deeper.

Cade sets a relentless pace, pounding into my aching pussy with abandon. The heavy table beneath us rocks with each powerful drive of his hips. Obscene wet sounds fill the room as he fucks me, mingling with our animalistic grunts and cries of pleasure.

"So fucking tight," Cade grunts, his fingers digging into the flesh of my ass. "This sweet cunt was made for my cock."

I can only moan in response, lost to the intense bliss radiating from where we are joined. Cade changes his angle, hitting a spot deep inside that has me unraveling. My walls clench around him as I hurtle towards my peak.

"Come for me, my wild rose," Cade commands, his voice gravelly. "Soak my cock with your nectar."

His filthy words send me over the edge. I cry out his name as I shatter, my pussy spasming almost violently around his pistoning shaft. Cade roars as my fluttering walls trigger his own release. He buries himself to the hilt, his cock jerking as he floods my channel with his hot seed.

We stay locked together as we catch our breath, foreheads pressed close, sharing air in the afterglow. Cade softens inside me but makes no move to withdraw. "My beautiful Bonnie," he murmurs, "I'll never tire of losing myself in you."

I hum contentedly, savoring the intimate connection, the heady scent of our lovemaking. "Nor I you. In body and soul, I am forever yours."

Cade seals the declaration with a searing kiss, a promise.

In this moment, the shadows of our pasts are banished. There is only the two of us, a man and a woman, our love a beacon in the darkness. And I know with utter certainty that this is where I belong—in Cade's arms, in this strange and wondrous life we've carved out together. A beauty and a beast, bound by a love that transcends curses and time itself.

Don't miss the rest of the Spicy Romantasy series! Go to www.authorkenzieskye.com to find out where to get the rest of the series and to get a free book!

www.ingramcontent.com/pod-product-compliance
Lightning Source LLC
Chambersburg PA
CBHW021136130726
47988CB00003B/1327